Farewell to the Farivox

Harry Hartwick

DRAWINGS BY
Ib Ohlsson

FOUR WINDS PRESS   NEW YORK

PUBLISHED BY FOUR WINDS PRESS

A DIVISION OF SCHOLASTIC MAGAZINES, INC., NEW YORK, NEW YORK

TEXT COPYRIGHT © 1972 BY HARRY HARTWICK

ILLUSTRATIONS COPYRIGHT © 1972 BY IB OHLSSON

ALL RIGHTS RESERVED.

PRINTED IN THE UNITED STATES OF AMERICA

LIBRARY OF CONGRESS CATALOGUE CARD NUMBER: 73-182115

This book is for Maryann, who will know why.

Farewell to the Farivox

If you had been a boy or girl living on the American prairies in the early 1800's, you might have seen something no one will ever see again: the Passenger Pigeon. At that time there were so many of these birds that when they took to the air they actually darkened the sky. And when they settled in a woods to rest, their weight bent the branches almost to the ground, for often a single flock of pigeons contained millions of birds. They were so numerous, in fact, that no one dreamed they would ever become extinct. Yet they did. Hunters killed them by the thousands, and after a while there was only one lonely pigeon left—in the Cincinnati Zoo. But it too died, in 1914—and then there were none.

Today, scientists are sure no other Passenger Pigeon will ever be seen. And yet there *have* been instances when, long after people thought an animal was gone forever, one more turned up in some out-of-the-way place, much to the amazement of the person who found it.

Take the Coelacanth, for example. This was a fish that everyone was certain had died out sixty million years ago. But only a few years back, in 1938, some men fishing off the coast of South Africa brought up another Coelacanth, exactly like those that had lived in prehistoric times.

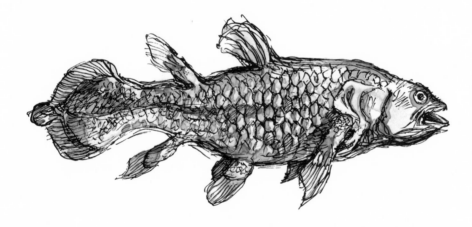

Or take ... the Farivox ...

Perhaps the last person ever to see a Farivox was a boy named Tom Elson, who lived in Vosburgh, Iowa, in the year 1916. At the time he was ten years old, and a student in McKinley Grade School there.

That particular Thursday in August began in a very ordinary way. At least nothing happened to indicate that before the day was over he would have one of the most unusual experiences of his whole life.

School was out for the summer, and there was really not very much for Tom to do—except what he pleased. And what pleased him most was reading. So every morning after breakfast, he went to his room, picked out a book from among the many Public Library books he always had there, and went down the stairs again to the front porch to read. For he was a great reader, a boy with a lively mind full of odd thoughts and fancies—a solitary youngster who lived much to himself and spent most of his spare time, not in games and sports, but in dreaming and imagining things.

On this particular morning, the book he had chosen to read was a short one, and he soon finished it. Then for a while he just sat there on the front porch, as he often did, chin in hand, and gazed off down the dirt street that ran past the house.

It was not a big road, in fact it was just a narrow little road in a country town, lined with spreading shade trees, mostly dusty elms and cottonwoods. But Tom thought it was like a busy highway on which the outside world paraded by him.

Sometimes an old man came along carrying all history on his back. In a great wicker basket he had white plaster busts of Indian chieftains, Washington, Lincoln, and many other famous men and women. He offered them for sale to the housewives along the street. Tom would think about the Indians, and Washington, and Lincoln for a long time after the old man had gone. It was as good as reading a book.

At around ten-thirty, as usual, the iceman's brown horse came clopping down the dusty road. The iceman, a big, muscular man with red hair, glanced out of his yellow wagon at the cards housewives put in their front windows to tell him how much ice they needed. Tom shivered, imagining how it would feel to wear a piece of rubber over your shoulder, as the iceman did, to protect yourself from the cold, dripping piece of ice you carried.

A little while later, an old man with a grizzled beard drove along the road, in a rickety prairie-schooner type of wagon. Under its weather-beaten canvas roof were boxes of soap, said to be made from an exotic plant gathered in scorching, far-off deserts. And occasionally Tom's mother bought him a bar or two because he got such pleasure out of using a soap made from those mysterious weeds. But today the old man, drowsing on the seat of his wagon, drove on past without stopping. And Tom watched him go by as the pots and pans that hung on the back of the wagon jingled and jangled.

The last one to appear that morning was the knife grinder in *his* big wagon. He stopped at the house next door, and Tom spent a few minutes watching through the open back of the wagon the spinning wheel that screamed so wildly as it spurted a thick shower of blue sparks. But after that, the street in front of the house fell empty and silent, until his daydreaming was interrupted by his mother's voice calling him to lunch.

Lunch over, he washed the kitchen windows for his mother, then set off to the Public Library to return some of the books he had had in his room. It was a bright, sunny day, a little too hot, especially if you stood still with your bare feet on the sidewalk. But a cool breeze was springing up, and he was not uncomfortable. He walked slowly, for other than the Library, there was no place he had to be until around five o'clock when he picked up his bundle of newspapers that the motorman of Vosburgh's lone trolley car threw off at the fire station for him. Then he and the other news-boys would take their papers into the firehouse and sit there folding them, so they could be thrown onto front porches. It was always a pleasant half hour, watching the firemen play cards, hearing the big horses stomp in their stalls, and listening for the fire bell to ring in the Chief's office. If it did, it was a thrill to see the gates of the horses' stalls snap open automatically, and the horses, without any urging, hurry out to the wagon that was waiting. Polished harness was suspended in the air for them to walk under. It dropped on their backs and was buckled up, and off went the wagon with its hoses, ladders, and pickaxes, while the firemen leaped on the back step at the last instant, still hurling on their rubber coats.

18

But picking up his papers was still several hours away. As Tom left the Library and came down Jackson Street, he passed the blacksmith shop and stopped to look into its dark, fragrant depths. The shop smelled of hot iron and dust. All over the place were the blacksmith's tools, and there were hundreds of horseshoes, clinging like layers of strange, sleeping bats to every surface, wherever you looked. The blacksmith himself, Martin Krebs, was working at the anvil—a tall man with a scrawny neck and thick, powerful arms, wearing suspenders over an undershirt, wrinkled black trousers, and a shiny leather apron. He nodded to Tom and smiled, without stopping his task of shaping a shoe on the anvil. Tom leaned against the rough, unpainted wood of the doorjamb and watched the flying sparks. As the hammer landed on the glowing metal it gave off a soft, crunching sound, not the clang you expected. The clang came when the blacksmith bounced his heavy hammer on the anvil between blows on the shoe, all in perfect rhythm. Then the shoe would be plunged, hissing, into a tub of water, and would be ready to be nailed onto the horse's hoof.

The horse waiting for the shoe, a gray mare, was standing beside the shafts of a wagon in front of the shop. Just inside the door, also watching the smith, was its owner, a fat man in faded denims, a nose covered with spidery veins, and pinched-up blue eyes. He was fanning himself with a ragged straw hat, very dirty and stained.

A slight noise came from the bed of the wagon, and Tom went over to see what it was. It was a scratching sound, like chickens walking on tin. Peering over the side of the wagon, he saw a battered suitcase held together with rope, and a gunny sack that he could see contained ears of corn for roasting. Up near the seat of the wagon he saw a rather large crate, roughly nailed together out of old lumber. It had slats across one side, and between them Tom could see that there was something alive and moving in it.

He went closer and leaned forward to look. The inside of the crate was dark, but there was something in there all right, something very odd-looking indeed. Tom couldn't believe his eyes. He blinked.

Its face was wide and flat like a monkey's face, but it had a long body like a weasel, with a bushy tail like a fox! Squinting his eyes at the floor of the crate, Tom could barely see the animal's small feet, clawed like a lion's. Its ears were tufted and sharp like those of a lynx, and it had a hooked nose like an owl. Between the slats two yellow eyes stared out at him with a soft, burning light—each one as round and golden as the little coin his father wore as a watch fob. Yet, for all their sharpness, there was something about the eyes that made him think the animal was actually smiling at him.

Tom looked at the fat man inside the doorway, who at that moment happened to be taking a pinch of snuff from a round flat box labeled *Copenhagen*.

"Excuse me, sir," he said.

"Name's Murray Bayliss," replied the stranger. "At your service, my boy."

"Is that your animal in the crate?"

The other nodded.

"I've never seen anything like him! What's he called?"

"Why," the fat man paused and slid the snuffbox back into his trouser pocket, "that's a Farivox." He spelled it out. In spite of his ragged clothes, he spoke like an educated person. "From the Latin: *fari* for speak, *vox* for voice."

"I recognized him," he went on, as if reading Tom's thoughts, "because once when I was very young, and going to school in Utah, I saw three of them together in a gulch. But the cowpunchers killed all of them. Very rare now—you hardly ever see them."

"Where did you find this one?"

"Well, now, that's very strange. Usually they live farther west, if any of them are left at all. How this one got into that cornfield near Warner City, I can't guess." He turned to Krebs at the anvil. "I just picked up a few ears of corn for supper tonight as I was passing a nice field. The farmers down there don't really care if you borrow some," he finished rather lamely but with a smile. Krebs smiled back and went on working.

Tom peered inside the crate. It was pitch black, but the yellow eyes of the Farivox still gleamed back at him. Suddenly he wanted the Farivox very much. "Would you sell him, sir?" he asked.

The stranger shook his head. "No, no, I couldn't do that. I've grown quite fond of him."

Tom was silent.

"Of course," said the man, rather suddenly, "I might have to, being a poor man and all that." He paused, and looked on with Tom as Krebs finished one shoe and began another which he lifted with tongs out of the flaming forge. "I was thinking of selling it to a good friend of mine when I get to Denison, over in Illinois. He runs a medicine show that travels around here in the corn country, and this animal would be just the thing for his show." He paused again. "It talks, you know."

"Talks!" echoed Tom, in amazement. "Really *talks?*"

"None better," said the fat man, and Tom could see he was perfectly serious. "As well as you and I. Or this kind gentleman," he added, gesturing toward the blacksmith, who was pounding merrily away at the anvil, the sweat streaming down his face. "You've heard of parrots talking, of course. Well, this animal, the Farivox, talks better. Animals, you know, used to talk a lot more than they do now. Even birds and fish. But they all gave it up. Probably found it wasn't worth it. Nothing much to talk about." He stopped, then went on. "Matter of fact, I don't talk much myself anymore. What's the use?"

"How much would your friend have to pay for the animal?" asked Tom, holding his breath.

"Ten dollars," said the man, rather sharply. "Or I'll keep him myself. Actually I get pretty lonely traveling around all alone, and this animal is good company. Says some very worthwhile things."

"Could he say something now?"

"I doubt that he would. He's shy with strangers."

"I see." Tom tried to remember how much money in coins he had in the cracked gravy boat his mother had given him to put on his dresser as a savings bank. It might even be that he had enough. Or if he didn't, maybe his mother would make up the difference.

"Would you sell him to me?" he asked the stranger. "I'd take real good care of him."

The man in the denim overalls looked down at him for a moment, then smiled.

"I might," he said. "If you have the ten dollars—which I sort of doubt."

"I don't have it with me, but I can go home and get it," cried Tom, and he started off at once. "I'll be right back."

"Hurry," said the Farivox.

Tom stopped as if he'd been shot. There was no doubt that the animal had spoken. It had said that one word clearly and exactly, just the way a human being would have said it, not gutturally as you might expect an animal to speak, or croakingly like a parrot.

"What did he say?" he asked the man.

The stranger looked a bit surprised. "I didn't hear anything," he said.

Tom looked at Mr. Krebs, who had been watching all this. But the blacksmith shook his head.

For a moment Tom hesitated. Then off he went for home, as fast as his legs would carry him.

Many years later, when Tom was older and worked as a geologist for an oil company in Abilene, Texas, he found that, like most grown-ups, he had forgotten a great many things about his boyhood. But he never forgot that afternoon in 1916. He remembered how he ran those six blocks to his home. An old man in a rocking chair on his porch stopped rocking and stared at him as he flew past. He fled down the sidewalk in front of the house where a surly dog lived that tried to bite him every evening when he passed with his bag of papers, on past the house where a rooster once *did* bite him as he tossed a paper on the porch. The surly dog barked madly as he went by, and the rooster took out after him. But he ran too fast, faster than he had ever run before, until he reached home.

"Mom!" he called, as he pounded up onto the front porch. He flung open the screen door and dived inside. "Mom!" But she was nowhere in the house—probably out visiting one of the neighbors. He'd never find her in time! Upstairs he went, to his room, two steps at a time, and grabbed the gravy boat on the dresser. It slipped from his hand, and the coins flew every which way. With a groan he started picking them up. Then, hands shaking, he began counting them. Nine dollars and sixty-one cents . . . and sixty-two . . . sixty-three. . . .That was all. But wait! Maybe there were more coins under the bed, maybe some had rolled clear over by the bathroom door and got behind it! He looked. Nothing.

Then another thought. Downstairs he leaped, to the kitchen, and hastily gathered up empty bottles he could return to the grocer. Putting them in a paper bag, he ran out the door, letting the screen bang behind him, and down the street. His breath was coming painfully now, but he couldn't slow up or stop. The grocery store was only a block away. He reached it, and flung open the door, so the little bell that usually tinkled now jangled wildly. The grocer, a small dark Italian, stared at him from behind the counter. He was a nice man, who now and then would buy Tom's extra papers to wrap food in—and once had given him, instead of money, a thin, black Italian cigar as rough and twisted as a piece of tree branch, which had made Tom deathly sick, and cured him of smoking for many years. Tom dropped the bottles on the counter. It seemed to take the grocer forever to count them. Then he handed over the few coins. They brought it all to just ten dollars and four cents. It was enough!

In another few moments, he was back at the blacksmith shop, half sick with breathlessness, but grinning triumphantly. And then slowly his grin turned to a look of horror. The wagon, the horse, the man, and the Farivox were gone!

"He said he couldn't wait," explained Mr. Krebs, shaking hands with the handle of a small pump behind the forge, and catching the cold water in a dented tin dipper. "Had to find a camping place before dark."

As Tom turned and walked away, tears stinging his eyes, it seemed to him that the light had died out of his life, as it was dying out of the late afternoon sky. When he reached home, he went upstairs and put the ten dollars and four cents back in the gravy boat on the dresser. Someday he would buy something with it. But nothing that he would want as much as he had wanted the Farivox.

As soon as school opened in the fall, he told his science teacher, Mr. Forbes, about the incident. He did it a little sheepishly and shyly, since by then he wasn't too certain about what he really had seen or heard. Maybe the stranger had been stringing him along a bit. The teacher wasn't sure, but he thought there had once been stories and legends about such an animal. Though whether anybody had ever actually *seen* a Farivox was another matter. Someone said the Indians had known of it. In fact, they claimed the Farivox had spoken Indian as well as it later spoke English. And in an old history book Mr. Forbes read that some of the earliest settlers in the American West had kept these animals as pets. The last one reported was in San Francisco, where one was said to have been kept in a restaurant for the amusement of the diners. But after the earthquake there in 1906, there was no further word of it.

In the weeks that followed, Mr. Forbes was interested enough to write letters all over the Middle West, trying to trace the man who called himself Murray Bayliss. But there was no money to pay for any real search, so in the end it was just as though the fat man, his gray horse, and the smiling Farivox had all dried up and been blown away by the dry August wind, like dust on one of Iowa's long dirt roads.

Many of the natural wonders that our ancestors knew and loved still remain for us to enjoy. But many other things they took pleasure in have almost disappeared—like so much of our wildlife. Diseases have reduced their numbers. Streets, buildings, and highways have taken away their feeding grounds. And hunters have killed them. Many of the most beautiful and useful animals that once roamed America seem to have lost heart and faded away.

Yet here and there, in the wilder corners of our country, a few of these lost birds or beasts may still live on. And every now and then, someone walking over fields or exploring caves and rivers may see, for the last time, the only survivor of some long-vanished species.

Or hear the Farivox say, *"Hurry."*